To my nephew, Pepo
—A. G.

For Hana Banana
—S. B.

Library of Congress Cataloging-in-Publication Data

Galan, Ana.
  Who wears glasses? / by Ana Galan ; illustrated by Seb Burnett.
    p. cm. -- (Scholastic reader. Level 1)
  Summary: Illustrations and rhyming text reveal which animals might
enjoy different sorts of eyewear, from fancy glasses for a snake to
swimming goggles for a shark.
  ISBN 978-0-545-21020-1 (pbk. : alk. paper)
  [1. Stories in rhyme. 2. Eyeglasses--Fiction. 3. Animals--Fiction.] I.
Burnett, Seb, ill. II. Title. III. Series.

  PZ8.3.G1215Who 2010
  [E]--dc22

2009032754

ISBN 978-0-545-21020-1

10 9 8 7 6 5 4 3 2 1   10 11 12 13/0

Printed in the U.S.A.   40
First printing, August 2010

Who Wears Glasses?

By Ana Galan
Illustrated by Seb Burnett

SCHOLASTIC INC.

New York Toronto London Auckland
Sydney Mexico City New Delhi Hong Kong

Glasses, glasses, all is clear:
what is far and what is near!

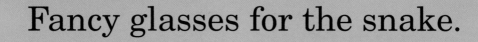

Fancy glasses for the snake.

Chimp needs glasses
that won't break.

Swimming goggles for the shark.

Tiger wears them
in the park.

Reading glasses for the school.

Lion thinks he looks so cool.

Big round glasses for the frog.

Hippo wears them in the fog.

Tiny glasses for the bear.

This giraffe just
wants them square.

Oval glasses for raccoon.

Little owl sees the moon.

Glasses, glasses, everywhere!

Glasses are so fun to wear!